The Tennis Ball Trees

Story by Christopher Lockwood

Illustrations by **Kathleen Fox**

The Tennis Ball Trees

Copyright © 2013 Christopher Lockwood
Illustrations by Kathleen Fox

ISBN: 978-1-938883-78-1

Designed and Produced by
Maine Authors Publishing
558 Main Street, Rockland, Maine 04841
www.maineauthorspublishing.com

DEDICATION

*This book is dedicated to Fannie, a very special dog and companion,
and to my wife Cindy (Fannie's "Soccer Mom"), with thanks for her support and inspiration.*

It's also dedicated to my children: Sarah, Nate, Aaron, and Joel.

To my grandchildren: Wyatt, Connor, Madelyn, Ellie, Dylan, Dulcey, Regan, and Ethan.

To the many wonderful dogs and cats who have enriched our lives.

APPRECIATION

*The author wishes to express special appreciation to Kathleen Fox
for her willingness to take on this project.
Her wonderful illustrations have really brought this story to life.*

Fannie is a Labrador Retriever—a chocolate Lab, like Fannie Farmer chocolate candy.

She likes bones and old sneakers. But the things Fannie likes most are tennis balls. She likes to have a tennis ball in her mouth most of the time.

Sometimes she likes to have two or *three* tennis balls in her mouth at the same time!

Fannie likes to play soccer. She uses her paws and her mouth. She wishes she could have played on the U.S. women's soccer team!

Whenever people come to visit, Fannie brings them a tennis ball. She likes them to throw the ball so she can run after it and bring it back. That's why she's called a "retriever."

Fannie likes to help "Mom" in the garden. She drops a tennis ball and waits for Mom to throw it. When Mom throws the ball, Fannie brings it back and drops it again. Fannie could play this game for hours. She's a good pal.

One day, a delivery truck arrived with a package addressed to Fannie. It was from her cousin Ike, a Chesapeake Bay Retriever who lives in Connecticut.

Fannie's family helped her open the package—which was filled with tennis balls! Fannie was very excited and happy.

In the winter, Fannie likes to play in the snow. She races around and dives to retrieve her tennis ball from the snowdrifts.

Sometimes, her tennis ball gets buried when it's left in the yard before a snowstorm. That's not a problem for Fannie. She uses her nose to smell where the tennis ball is. Then she paws through the snow to retrieve it.

One spring, after the snow disappeared, "Dad" dug holes to plant bushes in the yard. Fannie decided to help, and when Dad wasn't looking, she dropped a tennis ball into each hole. Then she scratched just enough dirt over the balls so Dad wouldn't see them.

Dad set the bushes in the holes and filled the dirt back in. Then he spread some fertilizer and watered the bushes to help them grow.

As the bushes got bigger, something started to grow on the branches. Were they nuts? Were they apples or oranges? What could they be?

Fannie knew the answer. They were tennis balls!

Fannie wagged her tail and pranced around the yard—as happy as any chocolate Lab could be. She had her own tennis ball trees!